OL' ONE EYE'S REVENGE

I'M ONLY SMALL, AND SOMETIMES TINY. I'M ON EVERY PAGE, CAN YOU FIND ME?

The yearly trip to Gloucester Docks to collect the cocoa was one of Dizzy Spells' favourite journeys. Jolly Boatman was excited too, as this was the first time he had been allowed to go to the busy port.

Muddy Waters told Jolly Boatman about how chocolate was made and why this particular journey was so important. As they passed through Stratford-upon-Avon, Muddy revealed to Jolly that cocoa had been carried along the canals for hundreds of years, and that was why all narrowboats loved chocolate so much.

'I need all the cocoa we can carry before I get to work on my special recipe,' added Dizzy Spells eagerly.

'This is one load I can't wait to get aboard,' said Jolly Boatman with a smile.

Ol' One Eye and his gang were planning and plotting. The pirate narrowboat blamed Muddy Waters for stealing his gold long, long ago. He wanted revenge and was thinking hard about his latest ambush. Pirate boats are very rude, so all that could be heard in their damp den was the occasional burblepop.

'That weren't me,' said Bish.

'Weren't me neither,' said Bash.

'Certainly weren't me,' mumbled Bosh.

'Boil yer barnacles!' shouted Ol' One Eye. 'Will you lot shut up. I'm trying to think.' The pirate boats knew that Muddy Waters and Dizzy Spells would soon be visiting Gloucester and that their fiendish plan was almost ready.

'My spies tell me they are coming for their precious cocoa. They'll pay dearly for their love of chocolate,' cackled Ol' One Eye.

Gloucester docks were alive with hustle and bustle when the Oxfordshire narrowboats arrived. Jolly Boatman asked if he could explore on his own before he picked up his cargo. Muddy Waters reluctantly agreed. He told Jolly to stay alert and not speak to strangers. 'Boats here are very welcoming and helpful,' said Muddy. 'But there are some that are too friendly with Ol' One Eye.'

Jolly had never encountered Ol' One Eye before, so he didn't understand what all the fuss was about. Just chatting to a few boats can't do any harm he thought, as he puttered off around the docks. In no time at all, he had told everyone he met that he had come all the way from Thrupp with his good friends Dizzy Spells and Muddy Waters.

'It's good to see you back in Gloucester,' said Willie the Winch to his very old friend Muddy Waters.

'And I'm really happy to be here, it's always so busy,' replied Muddy. 'Load on as much cocoa as you can, Willie. We need more than usual this year.'

'You need to be careful, Muddy,' said Willie in a low and quiet voice.

'Don't worry about me, I can carry heavier loads than most,' Muddy shouted above the noise of the docks.

Willie stopped the winch and whispered, 'Spies are looking for you, Muddy. Ol' One Eye is paying good gold to anyone who tells him when you arrive. You must go soon, but not the way you came.'

Muddy Waters had listened very carefully to Willie's warning. 'We have to leave and we have to leave tonight,' he said to Dizzy and Jolly.

'We can't sail at night,' said Jolly. 'Anyway, I've made lots of friends that I've arranged to meet tomorrow,' he added sulkily.

'Have you told them who you are and why you're here?' asked Dizzy. Jolly realised that Muddy Waters and Dizzy Spells looked very cross. 'I was only trying to be friendly,' he spluttered.

'Check your lights and check your cargo, we are leaving right now,' said Muddy Waters harshly. Jolly Boatman stayed very quiet. He'd never seen Muddy so grim-faced and he feared that danger lay ahead.

The three narrowboats sailed through the cold, dark night until they reached the 'graveyard of the boats', on the River Severn. The tide was low and through the mists of the morning, the bones of sunken ships could be seen emerging through the mud. Jolly Boatman was very frightened and he shivered as he passed into these new waters.

'I don't like it here,' mumbled Jolly. 'Can we turn back?'
'Shhhhhhhhhh!' said Muddy Waters impatiently. 'We can't see what's out there through this fog, so not a sound,' he added.
As they cruised further into the river, Dizzy Spells whispered a warning to Jolly and Muddy. 'There's someone or something very close and I don't think it's friendly...'

'Gotcha!' roared Ol' One Eye as he burst through the haze. 'This time there's no getting away!' he thundered as he rapidly closed in on the Thrupp boats.

There was no time to lose. 'Scatter,' ordered Muddy Waters in a desperate attempt to escape. Ol' One Eye and his crew fired their cannons towards the three fleeing boats.

Dizzy Spells had a plan. 'This way!' she shouted above the noise of the battle. Jolly followed closely, but Muddy Waters was unsure and confused.

Dizzy is taking us the wrong way. We'll be trapped if we go up river, he thought. There was no time to argue. 'I hope you know what you're doing,' he called to Dizzy as he followed her and Jolly further up the river.

Ol' One Eye let out a bloodcurdling cry, 'We've got 'em lads! There's no escape this way.' He let off another blast from his cannons. This is one battle I can't lose and nothing is going to stop me, he thought as he drew ever closer to Muddy Waters.

Jolly Boatman was struggling to get away from the pirate boats. The cannonballs exploded in the water beside him. Muddy Waters could have easily shaken off his attackers but he stayed with Jolly, trying desperately to protect him from the missiles landing nearby.

'This way boys, not too far now,' shouted Dizzy as the pirate's guns roared nearby. But it was too late. Ol' One Eye was alongside ready to take his revenge...

The first cannonball flew across the water hitting Jolly Boatman side on. 'I'm hit, Muddy, I'm hit!' he cried as he keeled over into the water.

Muddy Waters was filled with anger and rage. His engines gave a powerful thrust, as he rushed headlong towards Ol' One Eye's blasting cannons.

He knocked Ol' One Eye off-balance for long enough to get Jolly Boatman and Dizzy Spells to safety. Dizzy threw out her rope and lashed the Thrupp boats together. Jolly was badly wounded and in pain. He hoped Dizzy knew what she was doing.

'Why have we stopped, Dizzy, and why have you tied us to this tree?' questioned Jolly Boatman. 'They're almost on us again,' he added squeezing his eyes tight shut.

Dizzy smiled because she knew what was coming. 'Hold on tight, boys!' she shouted. 'This will be a bumpy ride... but not for us,' she laughed.

There was a sudden and powerful rush of water. An enormous tidal wave appeared and lifted the pirate boats high into the air, forcing them along the raging river.

'Whooooa! What trickery is this?' yelled Ol' One Eye, as he and his crew were forced downriver by the powerful wave.

'It's one of her spells!' screamed Bish.

'We're all going to crash!' bawled Bash.

'I'm taking on water!' bellowed Bosh.

The pirate boats were out of control as they headed rapidly downstream.

Muddy, Jolly and Dizzy all watched, as their enemies were battered and beaten by the raging river. All the rubbish of the river hammered into the nasty narrowboats leaving them tattered and exhausted.

'Let's head for the Kennet and Avon canal,' said Muddy Waters, as he led the Thrupp boats from danger. 'Ol' One Eye will never follow us there, so we should be safe.'

It was a narrow escape and Jolly Boatman was curious about how Dizzy Spells had managed to get them out of trouble. 'Was that a very hard trick for you to do?' an exhausted and wounded Jolly asked Dizzy.

'That was no trick, Jolly. No time for tricks,' replied Dizzy Spells.

Out in the estuary Ol' One Eye was badly damaged. 'They'll pay for this. I'll hunt them down and blast them out of the water. You see if I don't,' he muttered.
'Not if that Dizzy Spells is with them,' said Bish.
'Her magic's too powerful,' added Bash.
'Too good for us, boss,' piped up Bosh.
'Piffle!' grumbled Ol' One Eye. 'I know what happened here and I'll never be caught like that again.' he vowed.

Arriving in Bath, Jolly and Muddy had their battle scars seen to. Dizzy tried to answer the many questions Jolly continued to ask her. He was sure that she had used her special powers to overcome the mean pirate boats.

'You know, Jolly, there's not always time for magic and spells. Sometimes we have to call on 'mother nature' to help us out of a fix,' she explained. 'The Severn Bore is a force of nature, not a magic spell. The real trick, is knowing precisely when she's about to blow,' she added with a wink.
'Is now a good time for some of your real magic Dizzy, I'd love some of your famous chocolate?' he asked cheekily.
'For such a brave little boat I think it's the least I can do!' replied Dizzy. 'Now, how does that spell go...?'

Who is Muddy Waters?

Muddy Waters is no ordinary narrowboat as you'll discover in this exciting new series of stories. Set in well known and loved locations throughout Britain's beautiful waterways, you'll soon become familiar with such colourful characters as Dizzy Spells, Cedric, Dawn Chorus, Dudley and the rest of Muddy's buddies. Muddy invites you to find out so much more at

www.muddywaters.org.uk

Glossary

Cargo: things like wood and coal carried from place to place by the boats

Crew: a group of people who work together on a boat or ship. In this story, it is the group of boats that work together with Ol' One Eye

Dock: a dock is a place on the wharf where boats are repaired and where they load and unload cargo

Narrowboat: a canal boat less than 2.1 metres wide that is steered with a tiller not a wheel

Port: a town or city with water where ships load and unload

Severn Bore: a large surge wave that can be seen in the estuary of the River Severn at certain times of the year

Tidal: water that has waves and that rises and falls at different times of the day

Titles Out Now...

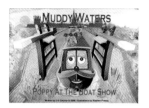

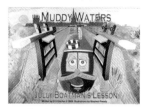

Poppy at the Boat Show

Pearly's Welcome to London

Jolly Boatman's Lesson

Hamish and the Falkirk Wheel

Coming Soon
Midsummer Milly and Cedric and the Bomb

Stay **SAFE** near water -

Stay **A**way **F**rom the **E**dge

wild over waterways

Go Wild Over Waterways - find games, learning and fun things to do at www.wow4water.net